To the memory of Rod Hull

Barefoot Books
37 West 17th Street
4th Floor East
New York, New York 10011

This book is printed on 100% acid-free paper

This book was typeset in Lemonade
The illustrations were prepared in gouache

Graphic design by Design Principals, England
Color separation by Grafiscan, Italy
Printed and bound in Hong Kong by South China Printing Company (1988) Ltd

1 3 5 7 9 8 6 4 2

U.S. Cataloging-in-Publication Data (Library of Congress Standards)

Hull, Rod.
   Mr. Potts and Mr. Betts / written by Rod Hull ; illustrated by Jo Davies. –1st ed.
[32]p. : col. ill. ;   cm.
Summary: Rhyming tale of Mr. Betts and his beloved pets who all get spots, and
Mr. Potts, the vet, who makes a potion to cure them—but which makes them
worse.
ISBN 1-84148-106-8
1.Pets – Fiction. I. Davies, Jo, ill. II. Title.
   [E] 21 2000   AC   CIP

Mr. Betts and Mr. Potts

written by Rod Hull
illustrated by Jo Davies

walk
the way of wonder...
Barefoot Books

Mr. Betts, who had lots of pets,
Went in a panic, one day, to the vet's.

The vet, whose name
was Mr. Potts,
Listened and said,
"You *have* got lots
And lots and lots
of pets.
What's wrong with
them, Mr. Betts?"

Poor Betts sighed and turned to Potts
And said, "My pets have all got spots:

A spotty fish.

A spotty cat,

A spotty snake,

A spotty rat,

A spotty rabbit,

A spotty frog,

A spotty canary,

A spotty dog."

"Dear me, dear me," wailed Mr. Potts
(And searched through his book 'til he came to "SPOTS").
"Now, strawberries suffer from *botrytis*.
It seems your pets have...*spottyitis*."

"Spottyitis? Is it bad?"

(Poor Mr. Betts was feeling sad.)

"Nothing bad that I can't cure!"
(Although Potts wasn't feeling sure.)

He thought
of pills or,
perhaps,
a lotion,

But decided
on a
special
potion.

He made it up behind a screen
And returned with a medicine that was –
bright GREEN.

"Give them this three times a day. That should take the spots away."

So Mr. Betts, feeling quite assured,

Was convinced his pets would soon be cured.

He followed the instructions to the letter

And wished and hoped his pets would get better.

The spots went at once! (which *was* a surprise)

But Mr. Betts couldn't believe his eyes.

He looked at his pets and shouted, "YIKES!"

No more spots...they were covered in

STRIPES!

Off at once, back to the vet's,
Ran an angry Mr. Betts.

"Stripes?" said an astonished Mr. Potts.

"You mean they've got stripes instead of spots?"

"That's what I said," said Mr. Betts.

"Now I'm the owner of stripy pets:

A stripy fish, a stripy cat,

A stripy snake, a stripy rat,

A stripy rabbit, a stripy frog,

A stripy canary, a stripy dog."

It was obvious something had gone wrong.

Perhaps the green stuff was much too strong.

"Hah!" said Potts, knowing what to do.

"Green's no good. Give them this...it's

BLUE.

With the blue stuff he'd gotten, Betts went away,
But you'll never guess what...he was back next day.

"Good morning," said Potts. "Did that do the trick?

Tell me your pets are no longer sick."

"Well," began Betts, as he faced Mr. Potts,

"The green stuff you gave me got rid of the spots,

But as you know they got stripes instead,

So I gave them the blue stuff, just like you said.

The stripes went away but it's worse than I feared...

Now each of my pets has grown

A BEARD!

A bearded fish,   a bearded cat,   a bearded snake,   a bearded rat,

A bearded rabbit,   a bearded frog,   a bearded canary,   a bearded dog."

"Hah! That's easy to cure, my good fellow.
Give them this instead, as you see...   it's YELLOW!"

So once again, Mr. Betts went away.

And once again, he was back next day.

"The green stuff you gave me," he said to Potts,
"Was quite successful – got rid of the spots.
But as you know, they got stripes instead,
So I gave them the blue stuff like you said.
Then, as I explained, the stripes disappeared
But left each of my pets with a great long beard.
So I gave them the yellow stuff and, by and by,
The beards went away...but they began to

CRY!

A crying fish,

a crying cat,

a sobbing snake,

a sobbing rat,

a wailing rabbit,

a wailing frog,

a bawling canary,

a bawling dog."

"Goodness me!"
Mr. Potts was
worried.
Again behind the
screen he hurried.
There, he thought
and scratched
his head

And decided on medicine that was...bright

RED!

Poor Mr. Betts, he gave a sigh.

Anything, he thought, was worth a try.

Taking the medicine, he ran from the vet's
But back the next day came Mr. Betts.
Mr. Potts was getting vexed
And wondering what would happen next.
Mr. Betts looked a sorry sight,
As if he had been up all night.

"Did it work, Mr. Betts?" the vet enquired.
"Did it have the results that you desired?"

"Well, the green stuff you
gave me, Mr. Potts,
Worked a treat – no
more spots.
But as you know, they
got stripes instead,

So I gave them the blue
stuff, like you said.
No more stripes but,
rather weird,
All my pets grew a long
beard.

So I gave them the
yellow stuff to try

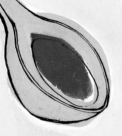

And all my pets
began to cry.

Next was the red stuff and it was no surprise.

They stopped crying at once...

...but they've

SHRUNK IN SIZE!

A very small fish,

a very small cat,

A little snake,

a little rat,

A minute rabbit,

a minute frog,

A tiny canary,

a tiny dog."

"Then we've won!" said Potts. "I think we can
Start from scratch – where we began!
Your pets are precious, I know you need them.
Now all you have to do is feed them!"

A whole week passed
And then at last
Hurrying, scurrying into the vet's
Came a delighted Mr. Betts.

Gone was his look that was always sad.

Gone was his coat that was always drab.

Instead, he was dressed in a suit, quite formal,

Proud to announce that his pets were NORMAL!

Happy now, he walks the streets

And tells each passer-by that he meets,

"I've got...

A normal fish, a normal cat,

A normal snake, a normal rat,

A normal rabbit, a normal frog,

A normal canary, a normal dog!"

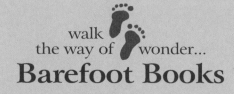

walk
the way of wonder...
Barefoot Books

The barefoot child symbolizes the human being who is in harmony with the natural world and moves freely across boundaries of many kinds. Barefoot Books explores this image with a range of high-quality picture books for children of all ages. We work with artists, writers and storytellers from many cultures, focusing on themes that encourage independence of spirit, promote understanding and acceptance of different traditions, and foster a life-long love of learning.

www.barefoot-books.com